O beautiful for pilgrim feet,

Whose stern, impassioned stress

A thoroughfare for freedom beat

Across the wilderness!

America! America!

God mend thine every flaw,

Confirm thy soul in self-control,

Thy liberty in law!

CHILDREN'S ROOM
PUBLIC LIBRARY OF NEW LONDON
63 HUNTINGTON ST.
NEW LONDON, CT 06320

W9-BMP-886

AMERICA THE
Beautiful

Katharine Lee Bates ★ Illustrated by Chris Gall

LITTLE, BROWN AND COMPANY

New York ⁊ Boston

JE
B

For my grandmother,

Elizabeth Keith Olmstead

Illustrations copyright © 2004 by Chris Gall

All rights reserved.
No part of this book may be reproduced in any form or by any electronic or mechanical means,
including information storage and retrieval systems, without permission in writing from the publisher,
except by a reviewer who may quote brief passages in a review.

Little, Brown and Company

Time Warner Book Group
1271 Avenue of the Americas, New York, NY 10020
Visit our Web site at www.twbookmark.com

First Edition

ISBN 0-316-73743-7

10 9 8 7 6 5 4 3 2 1

PHX

Printed in the United States of America

The illustrations for this book were done by hand engraving clay-coated board,
then digitizing with Adobe Illustrator for adjustments and color.
The text was set in Deepdene Italic and Deepdene.

About this Book

MORE THAN ONE HUNDRED YEARS AGO, in 1893, a young poet named Katharine Lee Bates sat high atop Colorado's Pike's Peak and was overcome by the vast beauty and unlimited potential of a young nation. It had been a long journey from her home in Wellesley, Massachusetts, and along the way she had marveled at the sights of a great landscape—from Niagara Falls to the World's Fair in Chicago and on to the soaring Rocky Mountains, where she now sat. Inspiration turned to words, and thus "America the Beautiful" was born. Two years later, the poem would be published for the first time in a weekly Boston church publication, *The Congregationalist*. The poem was immediately embraced by the nation.

Americans everywhere began setting the poem to music, and many different arrangements brought the words to life. The nation settled, finally, on a tune written many years earlier by Samuel Ward. Today, "America the Beautiful" remains one of our country's most revered hymns. The unabashedly affirmative lyrics speak of a nation blessed with God-given gifts and stunning landscapes—a nation built on law, idealism, and brotherhood.

As the great-great-grandnephew of Katharine Lee Bates, I grew up with a copy of her powerful poem, written in her own hand, hanging in the living room of our home. It was a constant and stirring inspiration to me as I developed as an artist. Everywhere I traveled I saw the country through the lens of the poem—not just its mountains' majesty and fruited plain, but its people, its industry, its inventive spirit. My goal was to create a dynamic visual interpretation that would reflect the soaring optimism of the poem while paying homage to some of our country's greatest moments in history. I could think of no greater gift to the legacy of Katharine Lee Bates.

Why does the poem endure as one of our most beloved national treasures? It is a reminder of all that we have, and of all that we need to preserve.—C.G.

O beautiful for spacious skies,
For amber waves of grain,

For purple mountain majesties
Above the fruited plain!

America! America!
God shed His grace on thee

And crown thy good with brotherhood
From sea to shining sea!

O beautiful for pilgrim feet,
Whose stern, impassioned stress

A thoroughfare for freedom beat
Across the wilderness!

America! America!
God mend thine every flaw,
Confirm thy soul in self-control,
Thy liberty in law!

O beautiful for heroes proved
In liberating strife,

Who more than self their country loved
And mercy more than life!

America! America!
May God thy gold refine
Till all success be nobleness
And every gain divine!

O beautiful for patriot dream
That sees beyond the years

Thine alabaster cities gleam
Undimmed by human tears!

America! America!
God shed His grace on thee

And crown thy good with brotherhood

From sea to shining sea!

About the Artwork

Lighthouses have always served as beacons of security, guiding wayward travelers to safety. West Quoddy Head Light in Maine sits on the easternmost piece of American soil.

Appreciation of the natural wonders of the land, great or small, begins during childhood.

In 1930, the nation was fed by more than six million small farms nationwide. Today, family farms have dwindled in number, but the legacy of America's agricultural heritage remains.

The view of Pike's Peak from the Garden of the Gods, Colorado Springs, Colorado. From the summit in 1893, Katharine Lee Bates was inspired to write "America the Beautiful."

For many, the change of seasons in a small town embodies the romance of American rural life.

Around 1805, the Shoshone Indian named Sacajawea—along with her son, affectionately referred to as "Pompy"—began to help explorers Lewis and Clark navigate the Missouri River and find passage to the Pacific Ocean.

Millions of immigrants from all over the world have contributed to the rich tapestry of American culture. During the country's densest period of immigration, from 1892 to 1924, most made the long journey aboard ships.

The travel trailer has given many families the opportunity to see our country's great natural wonders. Exciting stories about the pioneer Daniel Boone's adventures led to the popularity of the coonskin cap.

The statue of Lady Justice dates back to antiquity and has long been used to symbolize our courts. The blindfold stands for impartiality, the scales for fairness, and the sword for enforcement.

During World War Two, the men known as the Tuskegee Airmen were the first African-American flying unit in the U.S. military. They destroyed more than 260 enemy aircraft and won more than 850 medals.

The heroes of September 11, 2001. On that tragic day, more than 400 firemen, policemen, and rescue workers gave their lives in the service of their fellow citizens. New York firefighters pulled a battered American flag from the rubble and hoisted it high.

The Statue of Liberty stands more than 300 feet above ground and is perhaps our most recognizable symbol of freedom and liberty. Her torch is coated with 24-karat gold leaf.

The Saturn V rocket booster lifts *Apollo 11* to the moon. On July 20, 1969, Neil Armstrong and Edwin "Buzz" Aldrin became the first humans to walk on the moon.

A window washer takes a break on a hot summer day. Finished in 1930, the Chrysler Building in New York City has 77 stories and a variety of stainless-steel ornaments derived from the design of automobiles of the time.

Family time and leisure time are some of the great gifts that many Americans treasure.

On May 10, 1869, the East and West Coasts were finally connected by railway at Promontory Summit, Utah. The ceremony included the locomotives "Jupiter," representing the Central Pacific Railroad, and the "119," representing the Union Pacific Railroad.

AMERICA THE *Beautiful*

Katharine Lee Bates   Samuel A. Ward

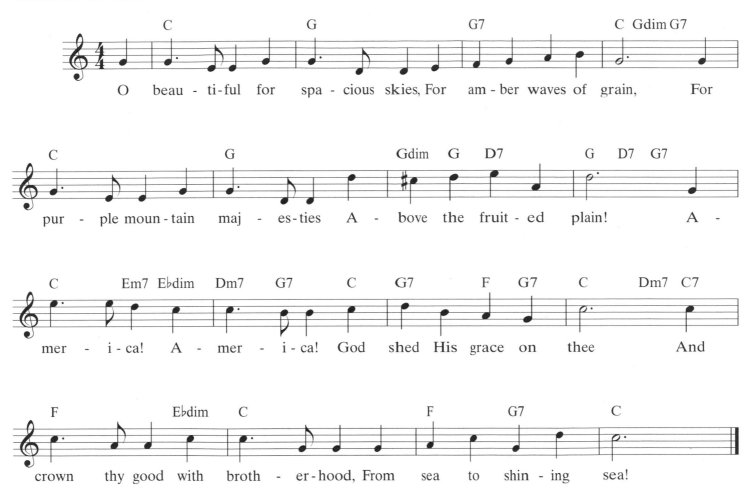

Public Library of New London
New London, CT 06320

A2130 168448 4

...utiful for heroes proved

In liberating strife,

Who more than self their country loved

And mercy more than life !

Am...........ca !

May G............refine

Till all .... nobleness

And every gain divine !

CHILDREN'S ROOM
PUBLIC LIBRARY OF NEW LONDON
63 HUNTINGTON ST.
NEW LONDON, CT 06320

12/04